DATE DUE

WOMBAT & FOX

Terry Denton

WO

MBAT
& FOX

TALES of
the CITY

Kane/Miller
BOOK PUBLISHERS

Kane/Miller Book Publishers, Inc.
First American Edition 2008
by Kane/Miller Book Publishers, Inc.
La Jolla, California

Copyright © Terry Denton 2006
First Published by Allen & Unwin Pty, Sydney, Australia

All rights reserved. For information contact:
Kane/Miller Book Publishers, Inc.
P.O. Box 8515
La Jolla, CA 92038
www.kanemiller.com

Library of Congress Control Number: 2008920673

Printed and bound in China
1 2 3 4 5 6 7 8 9 10

ISBN: 978-1-933605-81-4

Contents

For Jodie and Erica
You know what you did!

Wombat's Lucky Dollar

This is a story of what happened to
Wombat on Tuesday. I could tell you
about Monday, but nothing happened
on Monday. So Tuesday it is.

Wombat's phone was nearly out of minutes
so he went to the mobile phone shop.
He had never needed to get minutes before.
He had no one much to phone.
Except Fox.
Only Fox always had
his phone turned off
to save the battery.

"I would like some
more phone minutes,"
said Wombat.
The man behind the counter gave
Wombat a long hard stare. He snorted.

"How much do you want to pay?" he asked.

"Do I have to pay?" asked Wombat.

"Of course you have to pay!"

"But I don't have anything to pay with," said Wombat.

"No money! No minutes!"

Wombat sat outside cooling his feet in the
water that was running down the gutter.
"I want to be a millionaire when I grow up,"
he thought.

Speaking of millionaires,
Bandicoot drove by.

He tooted his car horn.
"Hi, Wombat," he called. "Guess who just
bought a brand new red sports car?"
Wombat ignored him.
"How come he is
a millionaire
and I'm not?" said Wombat.
"Stupid Bandicoot!"
He continued to paddle his feet
in the cool gutter water.

Wombat noticed something
shining in the sunlight.
On the sidewalk, to his left.

Your right.

His left.

"A coin," cried Wombat.
"A shiny, new dollar coin!"

He waited.
Just in case whoever dropped it returned.
But no one came.
So Wombat
picked it up.

He used the last of his
phone minutes to call Fox.

Fox sat upright in bed.
He coughed and a few feathers flew up.
Chicken feathers, I think!
**"Where's my
stupid phone?"**
he cried.

"Hang on, phone! I'm coming!"

As Fox ran, his big toe caught in the hem of his cape and he tumbled down the stairs.

He knocked over the hall table. The phone bounced off his head. Fox caught it.

"Yello!"

he said.

"Wombat? Why are you ringing me in the middle of the night?"

"It's midday, Foxy!"

"Oh!" said Fox.
**"Well, that's the middle
of the night for me."**

"Foxy, I found some money.
I'm rich!
I'm buying you an ice cream."
"Money?" asked Fox.
"How much money?"

Wombat ignored Fox's question.
"Meet me in the park in ten minutes."

"I'll have a lemon gelato," said Wombat.

"What?" said the grumpy man in the ice cream van.

"A lemon gelato," said Wombat. "You have to talk up, Foxy. He doesn't hear well."

"I'll have a double pistachio and vanilla," shouted Fox.

Then he remembered it was Wombat's treat.

"Make that a triple!"
"No need to shout,"

shouted the ice cream vendor.

"That'll be
ten dollars!"

"Oops," said Wombat. "I don't have ten dollars.
I only have one dollar."
"What!" yelled the ice cream vendor.

"Thieving animals!
Give back my ice cream!"

Fox panicked.
His hand trembled so much that he
dropped his triple pistachio and vanilla.

"Let's get out of here," said Wombat.
He and Fox ran along the path,
took a short cut through
the bushes and hid
under a bridge.

"Is he gone?" whispered Fox.
"Think so!" said Wombat.

The two friends huddled under
the bridge and watched the ducks
and swans swimming on the lake.

Wombat licked his ice cream.
"Want some, Foxy?"

"I hate lemon gelato," said Fox.
"I love it," said another voice. "I want a lick."

It was Water Rat in a canoe in the reeds
beside the bridge.

He tried to snatch
the ice cream.
Wombat pulled
it out of reach.

"RAT!!" cried Fox.

He jumped up,
and banged his head
on the underside
of the bridge.

"Ouch!"

Fox saw stars and
sat down again.

"You want my ice cream?" asked Wombat.
"Let's trade."

"No," said Water Rat,
snatching at the
ice cream again.

Wombat smacked him
hard on the hand.

"Ooowww!"
cried Water Rat.
"Don't hit."

Wombat saw the
angry ice cream vendor
hurrying towards the bridge.

"Here's the deal,"
he said to Water Rat,
"You give us a go in
your canoe and
you can have a lick
of my ice cream."

"A go for a lick? No deal,"
said Water Rat. "You must think I'm stupid."

The ice cream vendor stood on the bridge
and looked around.

"What about
the whole ice cream?"
asked Wombat.

"Maybe,"
said Water Rat.
"Okay, how about the ice cream
and my lucky dollar coin?" asked Wombat.

"Deal," said Water Rat.

Water Rat stepped out of the canoe.
Wombat passed the ice cream
and the coin to him.
Wombat and Fox climbed into the canoe
and quickly paddled out on the lake.

"This is no dollar coin!"
shouted Water Rat.

He threw
the coin at Wombat.
Wombat ducked and the coin hit Fox instead.

Right on the end of his nose.

The coin dropped at Wombat's feet.
He picked it up
and popped it in his pocket.

"Stop, thieves!"
shouted the ice cream vendor.

Wombat and Fox paddled
across the lake.
"Paddle faster,
Foxy," said
Wombat.

Water Rat and
the ice cream
vendor ran as
fast as they
could around
the lake.

As the canoe neared the other side,
Wombat handed Fox a rope.
"Guide us ashore, Foxy."

Fox stood up. His cape billowed in the wind.
Everybody watching asked,
"Who is that mysterious masked fox?"
Or so Fox imagined.

The canoe ran aground. Fox fell forward into
the water and got thoroughly drenched.

"My cape is ruined!" he cried.
Wombat fetched Fox out of the water.
"Let's get out of here, Foxy," he said.
They ran across the lawn.

The Hippo Sisters stood by their tandem
bicycle, thinking. They were always
thinking about going for a ride.

"Can we borrow your
tandem?" asked Wombat.
"No," said the Sisters.
"Wombat has a lucky dollar," said Fox.
"If you let us borrow the bike,
you can have the dollar."
"Show us," they said.

The Hippo Sisters looked at the coin.
"That's not even a dollar," they cried.
They threw it back at Wombat.

Wombat ducked and the coin bounced
off Fox's head. Wombat picked it up.
"It keeps coming back," he said.
"Maybe it *really is* a lucky dollar."

The ice cream vendor and Water Rat ran
across the lawn towards Wombat and Fox.
"Come on, Foxy," said Wombat.
They jumped on the tandem
and pedaled away.

"Come back with our bike,"

the Sisters cried.

Wombat and Fox
wobbled
onto the path.

Then off the path.

Then across the path.

"I've never ridden
one of these before," cried Fox.
"Me neither," said Wombat.
"Head for the gates," said Fox.
"I'll follow you."

People and animals and swans and ducks scattered in all directions. As Wombat and Fox passed through the gates, a lady with a pram stepped out in front of them.
She screamed.
Wombat slammed on the brakes.

The bike stopped.

But Fox kept going.

Over Wombat.
Over the pram lady.

Onto the grass.

Wombat
landed
on top of Fox.

"Ha ha ha!"

said Bandicoot, leaning
on his shiny red sports car.

"Bandicoot!" said Wombat.
"We need to borrow your car."
"Now, why would I
lend you my
brand new sports car, Wombat?"
asked Bandicoot.
"He'll give you
his lucky
dollar coin
if you do,"
said Fox.

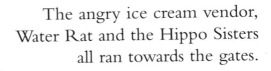

The angry ice cream vendor, Water Rat and the Hippo Sisters all ran towards the gates.

Bandicoot took out a small eyepiece and examined Wombat's coin. **"Hurry up, Bandicoot!"** said Wombat.

"Okay, my friend," said Bandicoot. "You have a deal." Bandicoot pocketed the coin and Wombat and Fox jumped into his car. They drove off just in the nick of time.

"At last we
got rid of that
stupid coin," cried Fox.
"That was my lucky dollar,"
said Wombat.
"Some luck," said Fox.
"Since you found that coin,
I've fallen down stairs, lost a triple
pistachio and vanilla ice cream, nearly drowned
in a lake, ruined my cape and
fallen off a bicycle. **That's the *unluckiest*
coin in the universe!"**

**"Where are
you going,
Wombat?"**

They drove through a red light and
down a one-way street.

"Turn left!" shouted Fox.

Wombat turned right.

Your left.

His right.

"Wombat, do you know
how to drive?"
"No," said Wombat.

"Stop
the car!"
yelled Fox.
"I'm driving."

The car lurched
forward and kangaroo-
hopped along the road.

It mounted the curb
and bumped into
a palm tree.

"You can't drive either!" said Wombat.
"I'm better than you!" yelled Fox.
"At least I stayed on the road!"
said Wombat.
**"You drove through
a red light,"**
yelled Fox.

"Hello," said a familiar voice.
It was Croc, out for an afternoon walk.
"Croc, can you drive?" asked Wombat.
"Sure can," she said. "Shove over, Fox."

Croc was a good driver compared
to Wombat and Fox.
She drove down the Boulevard,
the wrong way around
a roundabout

and through
a floral clock.

She almost ran over a police officer,

two dogs

and the lady with the pram.

"Good driving, Croc," said Wombat.
"Let's go sightseeing," suggested Croc.
They drove to the
Town Hall and listened
to the clock strike
three.

At the
Power Station
they watched
the steam clouds
billowing out
of the
chimneys.

Then they drove to the 24-hour concrete
crushing
plant.

Finally they drove
to Stop River,
under the Big Bridge.
The sign at the end of the road said,
"STOP
RIVER."

They looked up at the Big Bridge.
They listened to the traffic noises.
And counted trucks.
" … 112, 113, 114, 115," said Fox.
Wombat and Croc soon became
bored with truck-counting.
"Where is the car?" asked Wombat.

"Did you put the handbrake on, Croc?" cried Fox.
"What's a handbrake?" asked Croc.
They found Bandicoot's car floating in Stop River.

"It must have rolled in," said Wombat.
"I can't believe we didn't see it rolling," said Croc.
"I can't believe you didn't put the handbrake on," yelled Fox.
"What's a handbrake?" asked Croc.

Then a big ship cruised by,
and pushed Bandicoot's car
even deeper into Stop River.

"We'd better tell Bandicoot," said Wombat.
"He'll sell us into slavery," said Fox.
"He'll turn me into suitcases," said Croc.

They trudged back along the Boulevard
to Bandicoot's place.
Wombat knocked
on the door.

"Am I glad to see you!" said Bandicoot.
"Did you enjoy driving my new
shiny red sports car, Wombat?"
"Yes, but – " said Wombat.
Bandicoot held up his hand.
"Wait," he said.
"I have a surprise."

"You know that coin you gave me, Wombat?"
"My lucky dollar?" said Wombat.
"The *unluckiest* coin in the world,"
added Fox.
"It wasn't a dollar coin at all," said Bandicoot.
"It was a rare Transylvanian Tuppence.
And it's worth a fortune."

"Oh," said Wombat.

"Two fortunes in fact," added Bandicoot.

"Oh," said Fox.

"I am an even richer man now,"
said Bandicoot. "So I want to reward you,
Wombat. You can keep my new shiny
red sports car. **It's all yours!"**

"Oh," said Croc.

Wombat, Fox and Croc walked down
the Boulevard towards Fox's place.
Nobody said anything.

There was
nothing
to say.

Golden Cleat Fox

Wombat loves Wednesdays. That's because Wednesday starts with a "W"– Wombat's favorite letter of the alphabet.

On Wednesday, Wombat, Fox and Croc were practicing goal-kicking in the park behind the Oldmeadow building.

Wombat and Croc were
very good at kicking goals.
But Fox wasn't.
In fact, he was hopeless.

"Try again, Foxy," Wombat said.
"Just relax!"
"Relax?" said Fox.
"I have tried 123 times to kick a goal.
And 123 times I have missed.
How can I relax?"

Fox prepared himself for attempt number 124.
He took a deep breath.
He stared at the very center of the goal
and then he looked back at the ball.

Five steps back.
Five steps forward.
Fox kicked.

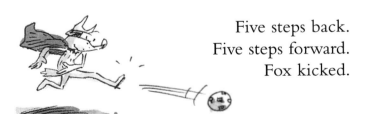

The ball flew towards the net, but at the last
moment it flew high over the
top bar of the goal.

Fox sank to his knees.
"NNNOOO! That's 124 misses in a row,"
he cried. "I'll never get the ball in the net."
"Yes, you will, Foxy," said Wombat.
"Just keep trying."
So Fox tried again.

"Number 125," said Fox.
He kicked. He missed.
"And another thing," said Wombat.
"Stop counting each attempt!"

"Maybe he has crooked feet," said Croc.
"Don't be ridiculous," said Fox.
"My feet aren't crooked!"
Croc and Wombat
studied Fox's feet.

"Maybe you're right, Croc," said Wombat.
"They do look crooked."
"Yes," Croc agreed.
"The right one
curves inwards
and the left one
is pointing towards
the rubbish bin."

"My feet aren't crooked!" cried Fox.
"I think Croc might be right," said Wombat.
"You can't kick goals with crooked feet, Fox,"
said Croc.

"Enough of this rubbish," said Fox.
He stormed back to the kickoff spot.

"Hey! Where's the ball?" asked Fox.

"Are you looking for this?"
It was the Five Monkeys.
They all laughed as the
oldest monkey
held up
Fox's ball.

He passed it to the second-oldest monkey,
who passed it to the middle monkey.

And they played the ball amongst themselves.

Around and around Fox.

And then
the youngest
monkey
kicked a goal.

Then the Five Monkeys ran off with the ball.
"Where are you going with my ball?"
cried Fox.
Wombat, Fox and Croc chased the
Five Monkeys through the park.

Croc, Fox and Wombat finally caught up
with the Five Monkeys at the playground.
They were standing on the fort.

"Give Fox's ball back," said Wombat.
"No way," said the Five Monkeys.
Fox stood on the seesaw
near the fort.

"Give me back my ball, or else!" he cried.
"Or else what?" asked the Five Monkeys.
Fox didn't have an answer.

The Five Monkeys
laughed at Fox. Then
they jumped off the
fort onto the other
end of the seesaw.

Fox flew up
into a very
tall tree.

He flew right up
to the top branches,
then fell back
down
through the tree.

"Watch out!"
squawked a bird
in a nest.

"I can't stop!"
cried Fox.

He crashed
through the bird's
nest, destroying
it entirely.
Three baby
birds tumbled
out of the nest.

Wombat and Croc stood
at the base of the tree
waiting to catch Fox,
but when they saw the
baby birds falling, they
ran to catch them instead.

Nobody caught Fox.

"NNNNOOO!"

screamed Fox, as he
crashed to the ground.

Wombat and Croc returned the baby birds
to their parents. At first they were very
relieved to have their babies back.

Then they turned on Fox.
"What do you mean by jumping through
our nest, you crazy fox?" they cried.
"We're ringing the police."
The mother bird took out her mobile phone.

"Don't do that," cried Fox. "It was an
accident. The Five Monkeys are to blame."

The bird started dialing.
 "Stop!" cried Fox. "What
if I find you a new nest?"

The bird closed up her phone.
"That sounds fair," she said.

Wombat, Fox and Croc hurried off along the
Boulevard and turned down Celestial Avenue.
"This is serious, Wombat," said Fox.
"Where are we going to find a nest?"

Under the overhead bridge
they met the Hippo Sisters.
"What are you doing?"
Wombat asked them.
"We're going to the
Boulevard to ride around
the roundabout," said the
bigger of the Hippo Sisters.

"Yesterday we rode around
it 143 times," her sister added.
"Until we got so dizzy we fell off our bike."
"Tonight, we are trying to break that record,"
said the bigger Hippo Sister.
"Why don't you come and cheer us on?"
"I might," said Croc. "If I can have a go, too."

"We can't," said Wombat.
"We have to find a nest for some birds."
"Fox wrecked their old one," Croc added.
"Why would you do that, Fox?"
asked the Hippo Sisters.
"It was an accident," Fox protested.
"It was the Five Monkeys' fault!"

"Do you know where we can buy a nest?"
Wombat asked.
"Try the secondhand shop on Tin Pot Alley,"
the bigger Hippo Sister suggested.

Wombat, Fox and Croc walked down
Tin Pot Alley to the secondhand shop.
"This is cool," said Croc. "It's full
of interesting stuff I need."

Fox found a soccer ball.
"Ha!" he said, "This ball is
better than the one the
Five Monkeys stole."

"Look, Foxy," said Wombat, holding up some golden cleats. "These might be just what you need to help you kick straight."

Fox tried on the golden cleats and they fit perfectly. He practiced kicking with them. "I don't think I need them," he said. "What we *need* is a replacement nest," said Wombat.

"What about up there?" asked Croc, pointing to an old mailbox. "It looks just like a little house and it's got a round door." "Clever Croc," said Wombat. "It's perfect."

Wombat went to the counter.
"Can you help me, please?" he asked.
"No," said the shop owner.
"I'm too busy."
"But I can't reach
the mailbox," said Wombat.
"I told you I'm busy,"
snapped the owner.
"Help yourself."

"Well, that's not
very friendly,"
muttered Wombat.

"Foxy, can you give me a hand?"
Fox lifted Wombat up on his shoulders.
"I still can't reach the mailbox," said Wombat.
So Fox asked Croc for help.

Croc lifted Fox up
on her shoulders and
Wombat balanced
on Fox's shoulders.
Wombat reached out for
the mailbox on the
top shelf.

Fox started to wobble.
"You are very heavy, Wombat,"
he said. Then Croc started to wobble, too.
"You are both very heavy," she said.

Wombat toppled forward.
Fox staggered back.
Croc's knees began to buckle.

And they all fell down.

Wombat caught hold of the top shelf
as he fell, pulling it forward.
Everything fell off the shelf.
And then the whole shelf fell over.

The shop owner ran
towards them shouting,
"Get out! Get out!
You're wrecking my shop!"
She swiped at them
with a broom.

Wombat, Fox and Croc ran out of the shop
and down the street as fast as their legs
could carry them.

They hid under the railway overpass until it was safe to come out again.

"Are you hurt, Wombat?"
asked Croc.
"No, I'm okay," said Wombat.
"What about you?"
"I'm fine," said Croc.
"And look what I ended up with."
She was holding up the
secondhand soccer ball.

"I am NOT okay," said Fox.
He was in a terrible state.
The mailbox was stuck on his head.
"Clever Fox," said Wombat.
"You've got the birds' new nest."
"Get this thing off my head," said Fox.

Wombat and Croc pulled

and pulled

and pulled,

but they couldn't
remove the mailbox
from Fox's head.

Just at that moment Bandicoot drove by.
"Hello, Wombat," he said. "Is that Fox in
trouble again?"
"Yes, Bandicoot," said Wombat. "He's got
a mailbox stuck on his head and
we can't get it off."

"You need something
greasy," said Bandicoot.
"I have something in the
car that might help."

"Here, Wombat, try this,"
said Bandicoot. "It's my new
invention, super-greasy
triple-strength hair gel.
It's made me even richer
than I was before."

Wombat squirted the entire
tube of hair gel through the
mailbox onto Fox's head.

Then he and Croc pulled
on the mailbox.

It popped off easily.

"Thank goodness for that," said Fox,
rubbing his head all over.

"Well," said Bandicoot. "I must go and make some more money."

"Thank you, Bandicoot," said Wombat.

"Oh, by the way, Wombat, you owe me twelve dollars for the hair gel."

"But I don't have twelve dollars," said Wombat.

"That's okay," said Bandicoot. "You can pay me later."

And he hopped into his car and drove off.

Wombat, Fox and Croc walked back to the soccer field.

Fox took the mailbox over
to the birds.
"Here's your new nest,"
said Fox.
"Thank you," said the father
bird. "It's a very fine nest."

Fox placed the mailbox
in the tree.
"A bit higher," said
the mother bird.

Then she took Fox by the hand.
"To show all is forgiven you must
share a meal with us, Fox," she said.
"Oh, no thanks," said Fox.
"I'm a very fussy eater."
"But I insist," said the mother bird.

Fox knew he
had no choice.

The birds served him
their favorite meal
– fresh worms!
Poor Fox had to
eat six worms.
And then a few
beetles for dessert.

After the meal, Fox joined Wombat
and Croc on the soccer field.

"I don't feel so well,"
said Fox.
"Maybe you've had
enough soccer for
one day," said Wombat.
"We can practice
another day."
"Yeah, let's watch
the Hippo Sisters
try for the record
at the roundabout,"
suggested Croc.

"No!" said Fox. **"I came here to score a goal and I'm not leaving until I do."**

Fox realized he was still wearing the golden cleats from the secondhand shop.
"Maybe these cleats could help."
"Good idea, Foxy,"
said Wombat.
He and Croc
sat down under
a palm tree
to watch.

Fox ran in and kicked the ball as hard as he had ever kicked a ball before.

It flew low,

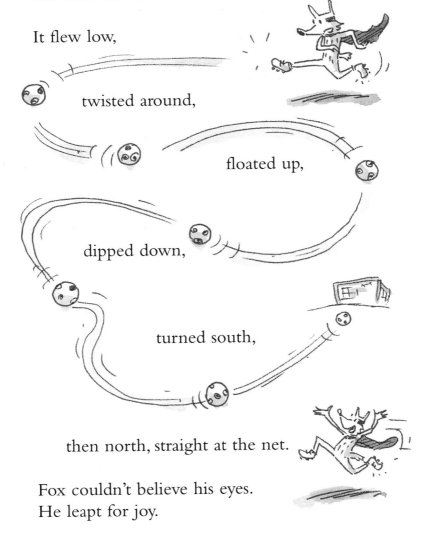

twisted around,

floated up,

dipped down,

turned south,

then north, straight at the net.

Fox couldn't believe his eyes.
He leapt for joy.

Alas, too soon!

At the last moment the
ball turned west and
flew wide of the goal.

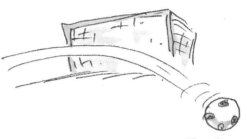

Fox slumped to the ground.

"NNNNNOOOOOOOO!!"

he cried.

"My 126th
miss in
a row!"

Fox tried to calm himself.
"These are *golden* cleats," he said.
"With these I cannot miss."
Fox tried again.

And again.

And again.

"I must be rushing it," said Fox.
On attempt number 134,
he took it very slowly.

He re-tied his wonderful
golden cleats.

He straightened
his cape.

He adjusted
his tail.

Then he lined up the goal.
Fox ran in and kicked the ball.

This was
the worst kick of all.

The ball flew
straight up in the air.
Very high!

It hovered for a moment,
then fell back down.

It bounced off
Fox's head.

This was all too much.

At last Fox did what I would
have done ages ago.

He gave up!

"I'VE HAD ENOUGH OF
TRYING TO KICK GOALS
WITH MY CROOKED FEET!"
he shouted.

"AND I'VE HAD
ENOUGH OF
THESE STUPID
GOLDEN
CLEATS!"

With all his strength, Fox threw
his golden cleats into a tree.

It was the
very same tree
where the bird family
was settling down to sleep
for the night in their new mailbox nest.
Fox's golden cleats crashed into the
mailbox nest and knocked
it out of the tree.
And the poor birds were
made homeless for
the second time
that day.

"AND I'VE HAD ENOUGH OF THIS STUPID SOCCER BALL!"

Fox kicked the ball into the lake.

Only he missed the lake.

The ball curved.

To his left.

Your right.

It flew into the GOAL!!!

"What?" said Fox.

"I don't believe it! I kicked a goal!"

And just to be sure it wasn't a fluke, he retrieved the ball and kicked it towards the lake again.

And again the ball curved
around and flew into the goal.

This was no fluke.

Fox danced.

And whooped.

And hollered.

And did handstands.

Fox ran over to the palm tree.
**"DID YOU SEE THAT,
WOMBAT?"** he cried.
**"I SCORED
A GOAL!"**

But Wombat wasn't there.
Nor was Croc.

Instead, there was a note pinned to the
palm tree.

*"Foxy,
Croc and I have gone
to watch the Hippo
Sisters riding around
the roundabout.
Good luck!"*

Fox couldn't believe it.
He had finally kicked a goal
and Wombat wasn't there to see it.

Fox was angry.
But he was also happy.

He was more happy than angry.
After all, he had kicked a goal.

Two goals!

"Just call me Superfox Golden Cleat," he said.

That night Fox slept soundly.
After 134 misses in a row, even though
nobody actually saw him do it,
FOX HAD FINALLY KICKED A GOAL!

TWO GOALS!

And you might like to know that the birds
in the tree slept soundly, too.
Fox's golden cleats made a very fine nest.

Two very fine nests.

A Hot Night in the City

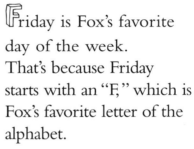

Friday is Fox's favorite
day of the week.
That's because Friday
starts with an "F," which is
Fox's favorite letter of the
alphabet.

This Friday was very hot.
The temperature
gauge on the
Oldmeadow building
hovered around
95 degrees.

"This is the hottest night in the whole history of the world so far," moaned Fox.

Beads of sweat appeared on his forehead …

… rolled down the furrows of his brow …

… ran down his long nose and pooled behind the black bit at the end …

… then dripped onto the carpet.

"Let's go
to Gorilla's place,"
said Wombat.
**"She has an
air conditioner."**

"No," said Fox.
"The Five Monkeys
will be there!"

"So,"
said Wombat.

"They are annoying!"
said Fox.
"I'm staying here."

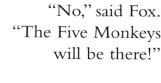

"But, Foxy,"
cried Wombat.
"They have an
air conditioner!"

Fox refused to budge,
so they stayed in
Fox's apartment
**and
sweltered.**

After dinner, Fox decided
to go to bed early.
"G'night, Wombat!"
"G'night, Fox!"

Fox lay
on his bed
trying to sleep.

But he
couldn't.

His pillow
was too flat.

Then too hot.

"How can I sleep with a too-hot,
too-flat pillow?"

Soon the bedbugs
began to bite as well.

Then mosquitoes arrived
and buzzed around
Fox's head, waiting
for an opening –
which they
eventually found.

"OUCH!

Stupid mosquitoes!"

Fox swiped and slapped at them.
He tried to squash them on the wall with his
pillow.
All he succeeded
in doing was falling
off his bed, bumping
into his bedside chest
and knocking over
his glass of water.

"Must have water!"

gasped Fox.

He staggered to the fridge, but the water jug was empty. There was no ice either. The water in the kitchen tap was warm.

So Fox staggered to the bathroom. The water is always cooler in there.

"ARGH!"

cried Fox.

"There's a RAT IN THE BATH! A HUGE HAIRY RAT!"

Fox
ran around
the bathroom
screaming,
**"RAT!
RAT!
RAT!"**

So Wombat joined in.
"Rat! Rat! Rat!"
they both yelled.

Fox stopped.
"Is that you, Wombat?
I thought you were a big fat rat!
What are you doing in my bath?"

"I was hot," said Wombat.
"So I took all the ice and cold
water out of the fridge and tipped
it into the bath. And I got in and
I must have fallen asleep."
Wombat and Fox sat
together in the bath,
until all the ice melted.
The temperature
reached 98 degrees.

"Gorilla's got air conditioning,"
suggested Wombat.
"No," said Fox.
"Okay, I've got a better idea, Foxy.
Let's go for a swim."
"Where?" asked Fox.
"In the fountain outside."

A few minutes later, Wombat and Fox rushed out of their building and on to the street.

"Last one in is a rotten tomato," yelled Wombat.

His fat little
wombat legs
were never going to
be faster than those of his
longer, leaner foxy friend.

Fox sprinted past Wombat and
took a flying leap into the fountain.
"NOOOooo!" he yelled.
"The fountain's empty!"

Fox landed with a sickening crash.
A puff of dust wafted up from the
dry fountain.
It had been a long hot summer,
with water restrictions.
All the city's fountains
were dry.

"Are you okay, Foxy?"
asked Wombat.
Fox's head appeared.
"You're a rotten tomato!" he said,
then collapsed back into the fountain.

"Last one in is a pig's bottom!"
called a familiar voice.
It was Croc,
running down the hill.

"Stop, Croc!"
Wombat yelled.
**"There's
no water!"**

Too late!

Croc leapt into
the fountain.

There was a loud hollow thud — like the
sound of a crocodile landing on a fox
who is lying on concrete.

And a puff
of dust.

The thud caused
plates to rattle in
nearby apartments.

Babies woke from
their slumbers.

Whole buildings
trembled.

And Fox's ribs
almost broke.

Wombat, Fox and Croc
sat quietly on the edge of the fountain.
The temperature gauge on the Oldmeadow
building glowed 99 degrees.

"Sooo hot," gasped Fox.
"Let's go swim in Gorilla's
pool," said Wombat.
Fox massaged his aching ribs.
"I want to go home
and sit in the dark."

Anything was better
than facing the
Five Monkeys.

"I'm so hot
I could eat
the top off a
fire hydrant,"
announced Croc.

"Now, that gives me an idea," said Wombat.
He pointed to the fire hydrant
across the street.
"Are you thinking
what I'm thinking?"
"Not likely," said Croc.
"It's Friday. I don't
think on Fridays."

Wombat crossed the road to the hydrant.
He climbed on top and tried
to turn it on.
But it wouldn't budge.
"It needs a special
handle," he said.

"Stand aside," announced Fox.
"This is a job for **Superfox**
with jaws of steel."
Fox grasped the top
of the hydrant
in his teeth.

"This is never
going to work,"
said Wombat.
"But it's fun to watch,"
said Croc.

Fox struggled with the hydrant until finally a few of his teeth fell out and dropped onto the footpath.

"My beautiful teeth!" he cried.

"Let me try," said Croc. She pulled on the fire hydrant. Eventually the heavy cast-iron top broke off and flew high up into the air, on a powerful jet of water.

Fox went up
with it.

Then Fox plummeted
back to earth.
"I'll catch you,"
cried Croc.

But at the last
moment Croc slipped
and fell in the pool
of water around
the hydrant.

Fox crashed to the
ground and the heavy
cast iron top of the
fire hydrant
crashed down
on his head.
It knocked
him out cold.

Wombat splashed water
on Fox's face.
Croc tapped him
lightly on the cheek.
"You have to give him
mouth-to-mouth,"
said Wombat.
**"Mouth-
to-mouth?"**
cried Croc.
"Why me?"

Fox's eyes flickered open.
"Hrrmmaa pphhaar brrr!"
he groaned.
"Are you all right, Foxy?"
asked Wombat.
Fox blinked.
He could see two Wombats.
He blinked again.
Now there were four.

A crowd had gathered, splashing around
in the large pool around the hydrant.
The Five Monkeys were there, too.
They were playing under the waterfall
and not making room for anyone else.

Then the Hippo Sisters rode up on their
bicycle, which had a new flashing light
and a new siren. And a trailer.
They were wearing Water Board uniforms.
They pushed all the people
back and put up barriers
around the hydrant.
The Five Monkeys
complained.

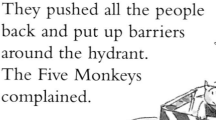

"Go back inside your houses," the Hippo Sisters yelled. **"There's nothing to see here."**

Wombat, Fox and Croc moved to the bench outside the supermarket. The temperature gauge on the Oldmeadow building had reached 100 degrees.

"I'm so hot," said Fox. "I wish I was a penguin."
"I wish I was a frozen chicken," said Croc.
"Clever Croc," said Wombat.
"That gives me an idea."

Wombat led his friends into the supermarket.
In the frozen food aisle,
he pulled back the sliding door.
"We can lie a
while in here,"
he said, stepping into the
frozen food
freezer.

"Not so fast, fat Wombat," said a voice.

"The Five Monkeys!" cried Fox.

"What are you doing here?"

"The same as you," said the middle monkey.
"Stupid Hippo Sisters turned the water off,"
said the second-youngest monkey.
"I was so hot, I nearly fainted," said the
youngest monkey. "So we came here."

"Shove over and let us in," said Fox.
"Buzz off!" shouted the Five Monkeys,
throwing frozen peas at Wombat,
Fox and Croc.
And they slammed the freezer door closed.

Wombat, Fox and Croc left the supermarket
and walked down Celestial Avenue.
It was now 101 degrees.
"I'm so hot," said Fox,
"I could eat an iceberg."
"I could eat a
polar bear,"
said Croc.

"Very clever, Croc," said Wombat.
"That gives me another idea.
Let's go to the Penguin Brothers Ice Factory.
They throw all the broken iceblocks out
into the backyard."
"This will be so cool," said Fox.

They snuck around to the backyard, quietly,
so they didn't wake the Penguin Brothers.
But guess what!

They were too late.
There were five blocks of ice with a monkey
bottom sitting on each one.

"Not fair," cried Fox.

"Too slow," said the oldest monkey.
"They threw us out of the supermarket,"
said the second-oldest monkey.
"So we came straight here,"
said the middle monkey.
"We took the short cut,"
said the second-youngest monkey.
"We hurried so fast, I nearly fainted,"
said the youngest monkey.

Wombat, Fox and Croc walked along the river bank, past the supermarket parking lot.

"Hello," called a voice.
"Hi, Gorilla," said Wombat.
"It sure is a hot night, Wombat," said Gorilla.
"Why don't you pop around to our place for a swim in our pool? The Five Monkeys would love to see you. They haven't been out for three days and they are getting restless."

"What do you mean they haven't been
out for three days?" asked Wombat.
"They were very naughty," said Gorilla.
"I won't go into details,
but they are grounded
for a week."
"Is that so?"
asked Wombat.

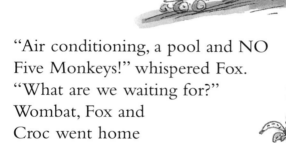

"Air conditioning, a pool and NO
Five Monkeys!" whispered Fox.
"What are we waiting for?"
Wombat, Fox and
Croc went home
with Gorilla.

She made
banana pancakes,
banana muffins
and banana
milkshakes.

With extra banana.

"I hate banana,"
said Fox.
"Can I have
yours?" asked Croc.
"I love banana."

"Are the Five Monkeys going to have some?"
asked Wombat.
"Poor darlings," said Gorilla. "They are
in their room, watching TV."

"Let's go for a swim,"
said Fox.
"Great thinking, Foxy,"
said Wombat.
"The water looks so cool."

"Last one in is a rotten tomato!" cried Croc,
and she leapt into the pool.

At that moment
the Five Monkeys
tumbled over
the back gate.

They all pointed at Fox.
"What are you doing at our house, skinny
chest?" asked the oldest monkey.
"Stupid cape," said the second-oldest monkey.
"Weird mask," said the middle monkey.
And they all laughed at Fox.

"So, my monkey friends,"
said Wombat.
"Gorilla told us you
weren't allowed
out of the house."
He fixed them
with his special
Wombat stare.

The
Five Monkeys
fell silent.
Then the oldest
monkey said,
"You won't tell her, will you?
She'll skin us alive if she finds out."
"Of course I won't tell," said Wombat.
"Unless I forget."

"Unless you forget what?"

cried the second-oldest monkey.

"Unless I forget to remember," said Wombat.
"Now we are going for a swim and we don't
wish to be disturbed."

"Anything you say,
Wombat," chorused
the Five Monkeys.

Wombat gave them one last special stare,
then he joined Croc in the pool.

Fox stood watching
the Five Monkeys.
They said nothing.
No sniggers.
No pointing.
No pinching.
No nasty remarks.

"Bring us some icy cold drinks," said Fox. He closed one eye and opened the other one wide, trying to copy the special Wombat stare.

"Right away, Fox," the Five Monkeys said, hurrying to the door.

"With lots of ice!" Fox added, giving them that Wombat stare again. "Or I'll tell Gorilla."

The monkeys hurried down the hall, tripping over each other as they went.

Then Fox smiled
a broad smile
and dived
into the pool.

A message from Terry Denton

I first met Wombat on a camping holiday.
It was love at first sight, even though Wombat
did steal my chocolate biscuits. Wombat is like that;
he sees something he wants and he goes for it with
quiet determination.

I first met Fox one night when he was trying
to steal my chooks. He tried to escape over the
back fence. He tripped and stumbled and eventually
had three goes at it. As he ran off,
he looked back at me as if to say, "I can do better. I
am a superfox."

These days Wombat and Fox
visit often to tell me all
about their adventures
in the big city.

www.terrydenton.com